DADDY

ME

To Frol and Jean,
future and present fathers

ABOUT THIS BOOK

The illustrations for this book were done in watercolor on eggshell textured paper. This book was edited by Allison Moore and designed by Nicole Brown with art direction by David Caplan. The production was supervised by Erika Schwartz, and the production editor was Marisa Finkelstein. The text was set in GFY Palmer, and the display type is Wanderlust Letters Pro.

Dad By My Side

Written and illustrated by Soosh

Little, Brown and Company

New York   Boston

With Dad by my side,
there's nothing we can't do.

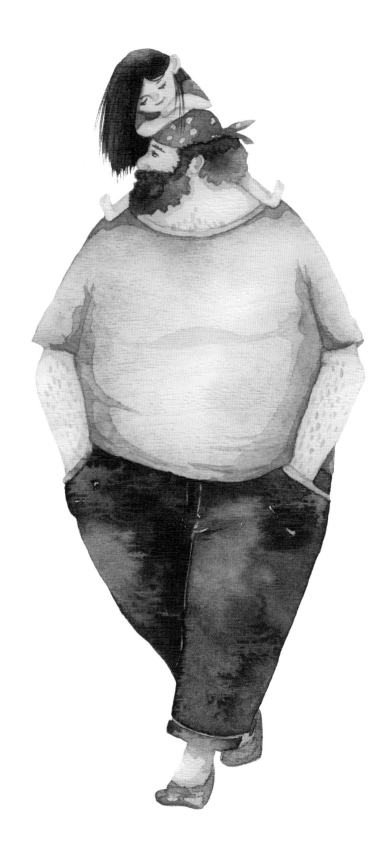

He knows how to make me smile.

He's not afraid to look silly.

No matter how busy he is,
he always makes time.

We love to try new things together.

Eggshells in our omelets
don't bother us at all.

He comforts me when I'm sad.

I make him feel better, too.

Neither of us likes it
when he has to go away.

But he doesn't miss a single lullaby,
even when he's far from home.

We fill our house
with special marks.

He teaches me.

And I teach him, too.

We love to cuddle.

He always makes space.

He tells the best stories.

He makes every room feel cozy.

He protects me
from monsters under the bed.

He helps me.

And I help him, too.

It doesn't matter what we're doing,
as long as we're together.

With Dad by my side,
I can reach the stars.

A note from the author

My name is Soosh. I was born in Europe, in a country that doesn't exist anymore. I have been doodling and drawing and painting for as long as I can remember.

My father-and-daughter series of illustrations came to me during a difficult period in my life, when I felt lost and unprotected. People were telling me to do something serious with my future, but I wasn't sure of my next step. Then I saw the father in my mind—this giant, kind, and loving protector, who can make all things possible.

He is deliberately big, much bigger than the figure of the little girl, his daughter, because this is how she sees him—and this is how many of us see our heroes or parents (which, if we are lucky, are the same thing). His beard makes me think of something ancient, strong, solid. He is someone who is there just because: to love you without any reason, unconditionally and forever. He is the kind of figure I hope I can be for my son, and one I hope he can be for his own children someday.

I posted my first few images in this collection online and was blown away by the response. I heard from thousands of people all over the world, relating this little family to their own and inspiring me to continue. I knew I had finally found my next step.